UNSOLVED
BIGFOOT

DINAH WILLIAMS

Children's Press®

An imprint of Scholastic Inc.

Special thanks to our fact-checker M. L. Liu

Copyright © 2025 by Scholastic Inc.

All rights reserved. Published by Children's Press, an imprint of Scholastic Inc., *Publishers since 1920*. SCHOLASTIC, CHILDREN'S PRESS, and associated logos are trademarks and/or registered trademarks of Scholastic Inc.

The publisher does not have any control over and does not assume any responsibility for author or third-party websites or their content.

No part of this publication may be reproduced, stored in a retrieval system, or transmitted in any form or by any means, electronic, mechanical, photocopying, recording, or otherwise, or used to train any artificial intelligence technologies, without written permission of the publisher. For information regarding permission, write to Scholastic Inc., Attention: Permissions Department, 557 Broadway, New York, NY 10012.

The publisher and the author have made every effort to ensure that the information in this book was correct at press time. However, we recognize that new information is still forthcoming and that the nature of this subject matter in part lends itself to theories and first-person accounts that can be problematic to prove.

Library of Congress Cataloging-in-Publication Data available

ISBN 978-1-5461-4157-0 (library binding) | ISBN 978-1-5461-4158-7 (paperback)

10 9 8 7 6 5 4 3 2 1   25 26 27 28 29

Printed in China 62

First edition, 2025

Book design by Kay Petronio

Photos ©: back cover background: David Wall/Getty Images; 2–3 background: David Wall/Getty Images; 2 bottom left: Jerell Ferry/Getty Images; 4 top: RichVintage/Getty Images; 6–7: Fauna/Roman Uchytel; 7 map: Juanmonino/Getty Images; 8: Rainer Lesniewski/Getty Images; 9: Dale O'Dell/Alamy Images; 10: Mario Solero/Flickr; 12 foreground: Dorling Kindersley/Getty Images; 12–13 background: Historia/Shutterstock; 15 top: Daniel Eskridge/Alamy Images; 15 bottom: Adisha Pramod/Alamy Images; 16 background: David Wall/Getty Images; 16 foreground: Valemount Museum and Archive; 17: Dale O'Dell/Alamy Images; 19: RichVintage/Getty Images; 22: Willow Creek China Flat Museum; 23 center: Dave Rubert Photography; 27 top: RichVintage/Getty Images; 27 bottom: Natalya Pluzhnikov/500px/Getty Images; 28: John Zada/Alamy Images; 29 center: R. Patterson; 30: Buddy Mays/Alamy Images; 31 all: Jim Mills/YouTube; 32: YouTube; 33 bottom: YouTube; 34–35 all: Stetson Parker/YouTube; 36: Victor Habbick Visions/Science Photo Library/Getty Images; 37 center: Bigfoot Global/LLC/YourTube; 38 all: C. Murphy;Murphy/Hancock Photo Library; 39 bottom: Courtesy of She-Squatchers; 40: William Moore/The Oklahoman; 41 all: C. Murphy;Murphy/Hancock Photo Library; 42–43: Brian Cahn/ZUMA Press Wire/Alamy Images; 44 bottom right: Eureka Humboldt Standard/Newspapers.com; 44 top left: Valemount Museum and Archive; 44 top right: Newspapers.com; 45 top left: Mills/YouTube; 45 top right: Stetson Parker/YouTube; 45 bottom left: John Zada/Alamy Images; 45 bottom right: YouTube; 46 bottom left: RGR Collection/Alamy Images; 46 bottom right: John Zada/Alamy Images.

All other photos © Shutterstock.

CONTENTS

INTRODUCTION: Bigfoot: Fact or Fiction?... 4

CHAPTER 1: Wild Beasts in History.........10

CHAPTER 2: Modern Sightings...............16

CHAPTER 3: The Hunt Continues...........24

CHAPTER 4: More Evidence.................30

CHAPTER 5: What to Believe?.............. 36

Timeline: Then and Now...................... 44

Bigfoot Fame................................. 46

Glossary...................................... 47

Index... 48

About the Author............................. 48

INTRODUCTION
BIGFOOT: FACT OR FICTION?

The world is filled with tales of mysterious creatures. Vampires. Mermaids. Unicorns. Are they real or imagined?

Vampire

Mermaid

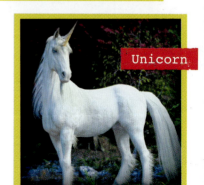

Unicorn

You have probably heard of Bigfoot. The beast is described as eight feet tall. It is covered with dark hair. Its face looks like that of an ape, but it walks on two feet. People say they have heard it howl. And some say that it smells awful!

Bigfoot

Gigantopithecus

If Bigfoot is real, where did it come from? Bigfoot could be a type of **prehistoric** giant ape. *Gigantopithecus* lived in Asia. It was thought to be as big as ten feet tall. Some believed it walked on two feet.

This map shows the location of the Bering Strait.

Scientists believe *Gigantopithecus* went extinct 250,000 years ago. Others think that a few came over the **Bering Strait** into North America. They could still be alive. But there is no proof.

Map of the Pacific Northwest

Bigfoot is a North American legend. Many Bigfoot stories come from Canada and the **Pacific Northwest**. These areas have a lot of mountains and forests. There are many places for this curious creature to hide from humans.

People have taken pictures and videos of Bigfoot. Footprints and hair have been found. But all of these things could have been made by humans to trick people. Is Bigfoot real or a **hoax**? Let's explore what we know!

This image of Bigfoot looks real. But it was created with photo editing.

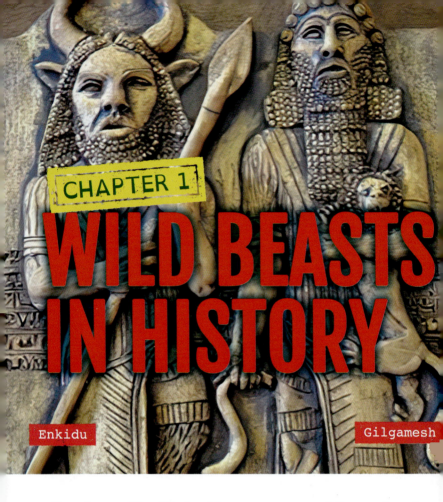

CHAPTER 1
WILD BEASTS IN HISTORY

Enkidu

Gilgamesh

Creatures like Bigfoot have appeared throughout history. One is described in a **Sumerian** story from 2000 **BCE**. He was a hairy, wild man named Enkidu. He had horns like a bull. He fought with a king named Gilgamesh. But then Enkidu and Gilgamesh became friends.

HOAX ALERT!

Stories from **ancient** times featured a lot of creatures that were not real. For example, dragons have been written about for centuries.

Dragons are still popular in today's culture. They appear in many books, TV shows, and movies.

Wild beasts also appeared in the history of ancient Greece. The leader Alexander the Great confronted hundreds of them in Asia. Some he battled. Some were captured.

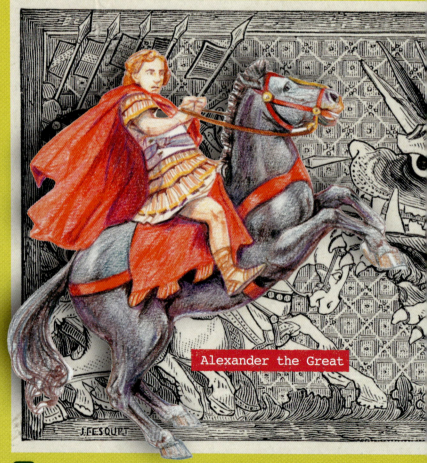

Alexander the Great

Nearchus, a friend to Alexander, wrote about the beasts. They were "hairy, not only their heads but the rest of their bodies." They had claws for fingernails.

Some **Indigenous** people in North America have long told similar stories. They said wild beasts lived in the woods. These wild beasts stayed away from humans.

They made stone carvings of a creature that looked like an ape. But there are no wild apes in North America. The apelike creature was later called Sasquatch. Today, Sasquatch is another name for Bigfoot.

North American Indigenous stone carving. It is of an apelike beast.

MORE LEGENDS

People around the world have also reported the existence of large, hairy beasts.

NAME	REGION	IMAGE
YEREN	Forest mountains of China	
YETI	Snowy Himalayan mountains in Asia	
YOWIE	Outback of Australia	

CHAPTER 2
MODERN SIGHTINGS

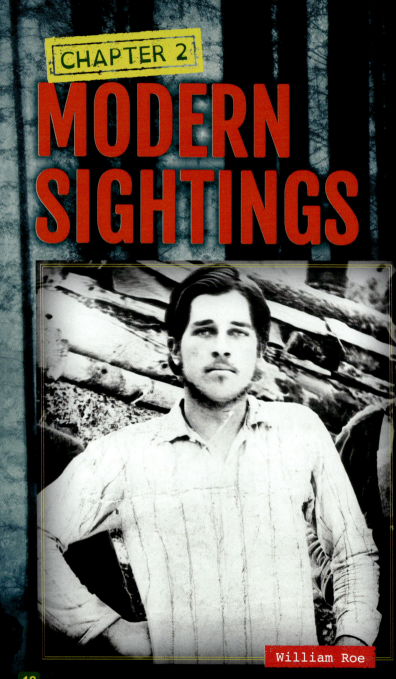

William Roe

In October 1955, William Roe was hunting in the mountains of Canada. He spotted a creature in the woods. Was it a bear? As he got closer, he saw "a huge man, about six feet tall." It weighed about 300 pounds (136 kg). Its body was covered in dark brown hair.

How would you feel if you saw a creature like this one?

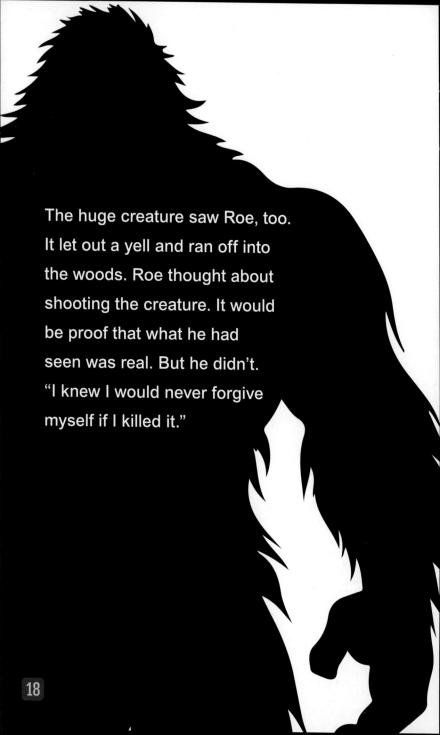

The huge creature saw Roe, too. It let out a yell and ran off into the woods. Roe thought about shooting the creature. It would be proof that what he had seen was real. But he didn't. "I knew I would never forgive myself if I killed it."

This image of Bigfoot has no source or date. Do you think it's real?

Crew claims he saw footprints. They looked like this one.

Three years went by. A man named Jerry Crew was working in the woods in California. One day, he saw huge footprints in the mud.

They were 16 inches (41 cm) long. Men he worked with said they saw the same prints in other places. Crew decided to call the newspaper.

Jerry Crew made a **cast** from one of the footprints.

The story ran on the front page of the local paper. It called the creature "Bigfoot." Newspapers all over the country ran the story. Soon people traveled to California. They wanted to find Bigfoot.

HOAX ALERT!

Dale Lee Wallace
(Ray Wallace's nephew)

Ray Wallace worked with Jerry Crew. Wallace told his family that *he* had made the footprints himself. After Wallace died, his family told the secret. In the photo, Wallace's nephew is holding two fake feet. He said Ray used them to make the footprints. Still, some people didn't believe him.

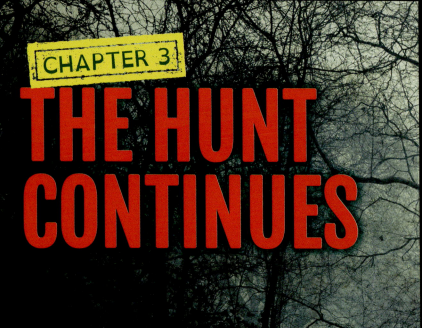

CHAPTER 3
THE HUNT CONTINUES

Hundreds of people reported seeing Bigfoot over the next few years. Most of their stories are hard to believe. But some could be true.

It was nighttime in California in 1962. Robert Hatfield heard dogs barking in the backyard. He went to see why. Hatfield claimed to see Bigfoot standing near the fence. He woke up his brother-in-law. They went into the yard to get a closer look. Hatfield ran right into the creature! Bigfoot knocked him down.

This muddy handprint looks like the one left on Hatfield's door.

Hatfield and his brother-in-law ran back into the house. The creature followed them. It pushed at the front door before running away. The police came the next day. They found a giant muddy handprint on the door. There was a terrible smell in the air. Broken branches were found outside.

HOAX ALERT!

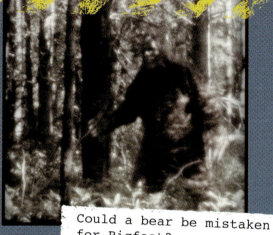

Could a bear be mistaken for Bigfoot?

Some believe what Hatfield and his brother-in-law actually saw was a bear. What do you think?

In 1967, Roger Patterson and Bob Gimlin decided to look for Bigfoot. They traveled to California. They rode their horses through the woods. The pair saw something moving by a river. It was Bigfoot! Patterson grabbed his video camera. He shot one minute of film of the creature. The movie showed Bigfoot standing and walking away. They had proof that the creature was real!

Stills from the famous 1967 Patterson-Gimlin film.

HOAX ALERT!

A man said he sold Patterson a gorilla costume. People who studied the film don't believe Patterson. Do you?

Robert Patterson made casts from the Bigfoot prints in 1967.

CHAPTER 4
MORE EVIDENCE

More than thirty years passed. Thousands of Bigfoot sightings were reported. One was from Jim Mills in 2001. He went hiking with a group in California. They stopped in the Marble Mountain forest.

The group noticed a creature walking at the top of a nearby hill. Mills took a video of it. The creature seemed upset. Was it Bigfoot?

Stills from the 2001 Mills video taken at Marble Mountain.

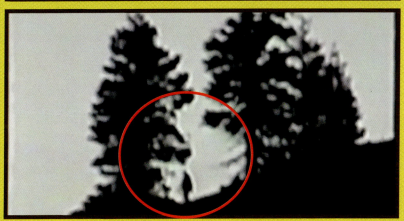

An image from the campers' 2012 sighting in Provo.

Many people in Provo, Utah, have also claimed to see Bigfoot. Campers in 2012 saw what they thought was a bear. They started to film it. Then it stood up on two legs and walked like a man. They were terrified and ran away.

There was another sighting in Provo in 2019. Again, a video was taken. The creature was far away and hard to see. What do you think it was?

The 2019 Provo video was posted online. You can hear someone say, "Seriously, look how big it is!"

Stetson Parker took a train ride through Colorado in 2023. Out his window, he spotted a tall, hairy creature. It had long arms.

Stills from the 2023 train sighting in Colorado. Do any of these images look like Bigfoot to you?

Another passenger took a video. "It didn't move like a person," Parker told a newspaper. He also said, "It looked more like an ape. I don't think it was a hoax."

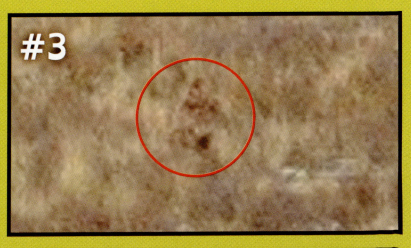

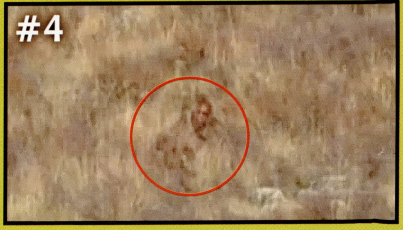

CHAPTER 5
WHAT TO BELIEVE?

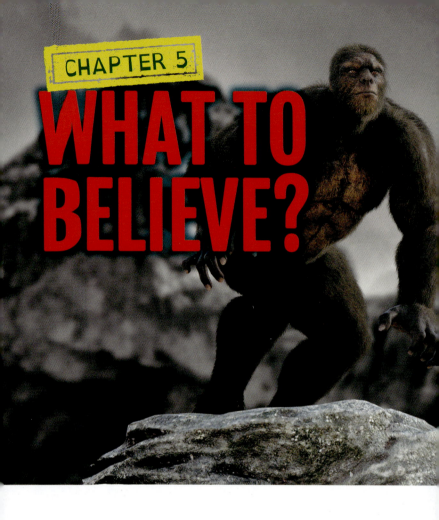

Why hasn't anyone found Bigfoot bones? Or a dead Bigfoot? Some people believe the creatures bury the bodies of their deceased. Others think it's because they live in caves. The bodies are harder to find inside caves.

HOAX ALERT!

In 2008, two men claimed to have found a dead Bigfoot. The huge creature looked like it was part man and part ape. They sold its frozen body for $50,000. But it was a hoax. The body was made of rubber.

This giant rubber suit was the fake Bigfoot.

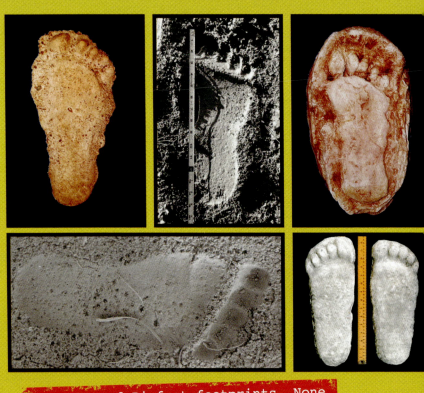

Examples of Bigfoot footprints. None of these match humans or animals.

People have been looking for Bigfoot for a long time. But still, there is not enough proof it exists. For example, thousands of footprints have been found. They are usually between 16 and 23 inches (41 and 58 cm) long. They are far too big to be human prints. And they don't match any known animals. But footprints are easy to fake!

SHE-SQUATCHERS

She-Squatchers is an all-female group searching for Bigfoot. They investigate sightings in the American Midwest. Why all women? Because they think Bigfoot is more likely to interact with a woman!

People also claim to have found hair from Bigfoot. In 2014, a group of scientists tested thirty "Bigfoot" hair samples. All samples were confirmed to be from known animals. They came from horses, wolves, dogs, cows, raccoons, and deer. One sample was from an extinct type of polar bear!

This Bigfoot hair sample was supposedly found in 2008. Which animal do you think it belongs to?

ANIMAL HAIR SAMPLES

These museum hair samples were claimed to be from Bigfoot. But they were all confirmed to come from known animals.

Items from the Sasquatch Museum in Blue Ridge, Georgia.

Some people find it hard to decide whether to believe in Bigfoot. It is important to question what we do know. Why? Because people lie. Some want to become famous with fake videos. Others want to make money selling what they say is "real" proof.

The mystery of Bigfoot will remain unsolved until there is more evidence. What do you believe? Is there enough proof for you to decide? Maybe you're not sure. Maybe we can all agree that Bigfoot is an incredible story, real or not!

TIMELINE: Then and Now

William Roe's sighting.

Robert Hatfield's backyard encounter.

1955   **1958**   **1962**

Jerry Crew discovers footprints.

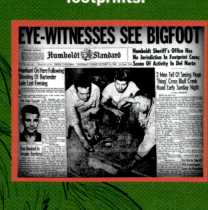

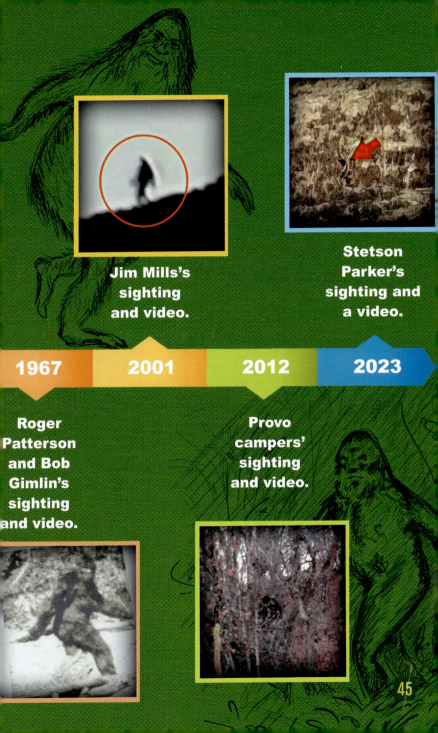

BIGFOOT FAME

Did you know about Bigfoot before you picked up this book? Bigfoot is still popular today! *Harry and the Hendersons* is a movie about Bigfoot moving in with a family. There is a TV show about people who look for proof called *Finding Bigfoot*. Some towns in the Pacific Northwest hold Bigfoot festivals every year. Where will Bigfoot pop up next?

Finding Bigfoot

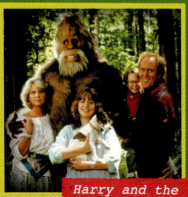

Harry and the Hendersons

Bigfoot festival

GLOSSARY

ancient (AYN-shuhnt) belonging to a period long ago

BCE "Before the Common Era," used to refer to the years that came before the birth of Jesus Christ

Bering Strait (BAIR-ing STRAYT) a narrow waterway between Russia and Alaska that many believe was once a land bridge

cast (kast) to form something by pouring soft or liquid material into a mold

hoax (hohks) a trick that makes people believe something that is not true

Indigenous (in-DI-juh-nuhs) of or relating to the first people to live in a place

Pacific Northwest (puh-SIF-ik north-WEST) the states of Oregon, Washington, and Idaho, and southern Canada near the Pacific Ocean

prehistoric (pree-hi-STOR-ik) belonging to a time before history was recorded in written form

Sumerian (soo-MEH-ree-uhn) an ancient people who lived in what is now southern Iraq

INDEX

A
Alexander the Great, 12–13
ancient stories, 11
apes, 5, 6–7, 14, 35, 37

B
BCE, 10
bears, 17, 27, 32, 40–41
Bering Strait, 7
Bigfoot
 body of, 36–37
 fame of, 46
 footprints of, 20–23, 29, 38, 44
 hair of, 5, 8, 17, 40–41
 handprints of, 26
 photos of, 8–9, 19
 smell of, 5, 26
 sounds of, 18
 videos of, 28, 30–35

C
casts, 22, 29
Crew, Jerry, 20–23, 44

D
dragons, 11

E
Enkidu, 10

G
Gigantopithecus, 6–7
Gilgamesh, 10
Gimlin, Bob, 28, 45

H
Hatfield, Robert, 24–27, 44
hoaxes, 8, 35, 37

I
Indigenous people, 14

M
Mills, Jim, 30–31, 45

N
Nearchus, 13

P
Pacific Northwest, 8

Parker, Stetson, 34–35, 45
Patterson, Robert, 28–29, 45
prehistoric apes, 6–7

R
Roe, William, 16–18, 44

S
Sasquatch, 14
Sasquatch Museum, 42–43
She-Squatchers, 39
Sumerians, 10

W
Wallace, Dale Lee, 23
Wallace, Ray, 23

Y
Yeren, 15
Yeti, 15
Yowie, 15

ABOUT THE AUTHOR

Dinah Williams, who loves all things spooky and mysterious, has written more than a dozen books for kids, including *Amazing Immortals*; *Terrible But True: Awful Events in American History*; *True Hauntings: Deadly Disasters*; and *Spooky Cemeteries*, which won a 2009 Children's Choice Book of the Year Award.